A JUST ONE MORE BOOK
Just For You

The Penguins Paint

by Valerie Tripp

Illustrated by Sandra Cox Kalthoff

Developed by The Hampton-Brown Company, Inc.

CHILDRENS PRESS ®

CHICAGO

Word List

Give children books they can read by themselves, and they'll always ask for JUST ONE MORE. This book is written with 82 of the most basic words in our language, all repeated in an appealing rhythm and rhyme.

a	get	new	that
all	grandma	night	the
and	grass	nose	them
are	green		then
as		on	they
at	hay	one	to
	he		too
best		paint(ed)	tree
black	I	passing	
blue	in	penguin(s)	uncle
blows	is	Penny	
bought			wall
but	just	rainbow	walk
by		red	wanted
	know		was
color(s)		said	we
corn	leaves	sea	went
	let's	she	whales
day	like(d)	sky	what
do		snow	which
don't	many	so	white
	more	spring	wind
fall	Mrs.	store	world
fine		sun	
fish		swims	yellow
fox			

Library of Congress Cataloging-in-Publication Data

Tripp, Valerie, 1951-
  The Penguins paint.

  Summary: The Penguins tire of their black and white world and decide to make things more colorful.
  [1. Penguins—Fiction. 2. Color—Fiction.
3. Stories in rhyme] I. Kalthoff, Sandra Cox, ill.
PZ8.3.T698Pe   1987   [E]   87-14081
ISBN 0-516-01567-2

The Penguins' world
was black and white,
white as snow,
black as night.

But all the Penguins
wanted more.
So they went on a walk
to the new paint store.

Let's get a color
we all like
and color all
the black and white!

The penguins paint.
Blue as the sea,

Blue as the sky,
Blue as the whales passing by.

But Uncle Penguin
wanted more.

So he bought GREEN
at the new paint store.

The penguins paint.
Green as the grass,

Green as a tree,
Green as a fish that swims in the sea.

11

But Mrs. Penguin
wanted more.

So she bought YELLOW
at the new paint store.

The penguins paint.
Yellow as corn,

Yellow as hay,
Yellow as sun on a fine spring day.

But Grandma Penguin
wanted JUST ONE MORE.

So she bought RED
at the new paint store.

The penguins paint.

Red as a fox, red as a nose,

Red as the leaves
a fall wind blows.

So many colors
are on the wall.
Which one is best?
We like them all.

We like the green.
We like red, too.
We like yellow,
and we all like blue.

We just don't know
WHAT to do!

Then Penny Penguin said:
I KNOW!
We liked them ALL
and painted....

. . .a RAINBOW!

24